TWELVE MINIATURES FOR FESTIVE OCCASIONS

NOEL
RAWSTHORNE

ORGAN

TWELVE MINIATURES FOR FESTIVE OCCASIONS

NOEL RAWSTHORNE

ORGAN

Kevin Mayhew

We hope you enjoy the music in *Twelve Miniatures for Festive Occasions*.
Further copies of this and other books in the series are available
from your local music shop or Christian bookshop.

In case of difficulty, please contact the publisher direct by writing to:

The Sales Department
KEVIN MAYHEW LTD
Buxhall
Stowmarket
Suffolk IP14 3BW

Phone 01449 737978
Fax 01449 737834
E-mail info@kevinmayhewltd.com

Please ask for our complete catalogue of outstanding Church Music.

First published in Great Britain in 1999 by Kevin Mayhew Ltd.

© Copyright 1999 Kevin Mayhew Ltd.

ISBN 1 84003 423 8
ISMN M 57004 588 4
Catalogue No: 1400213

0 1 2 3 4 5 6 7 8 9

Cover designed by Jaquetta Sergeant

Music Editor and Setter: Donald Thomson
Proof-reader: Kate Gallaher

Printed and bound in Great Britain

Contents

Noel Rawsthorne (*b*.1929) was Organist of Liverpool Cathedral for twenty-five years and City Organist and Artistic Director at St George's Hall, Liverpool. He was also Senior Lecturer in Music at St Katherine's College, Liverpool, until his retirement in 1993 after thirty-nine years in education. In 1994 he was honoured by the University of Liverpool with an honorary degree of Doctor of Music.

ALLEGRO FESTIVO

Noel Rawsthorne

VERY RHYTHMICALLY

Molto ritmico (♩ = c.120)

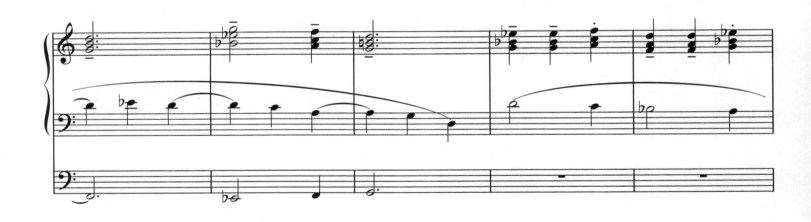

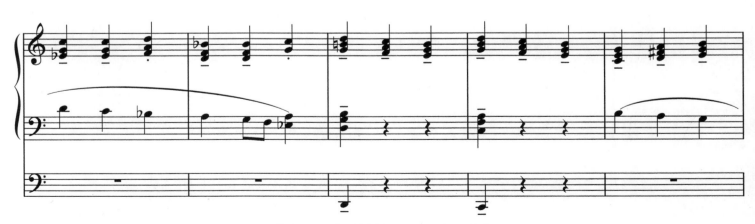

9

poco rall.

a tempo

10

MILLENNIUM PRELUDE

poco allargando

Full

ALLELUIAS

Lights glistening morn bedecks the skies!

* 'Lasst uns erfreuen'

ENTRADA

19

21

EXULTEMUS

Reduce *f*

JUBILATE

MENUET

MARCHE TRIOMPHALE

Full Sw.
Gt. to Mix.
Ped. 16' 8'

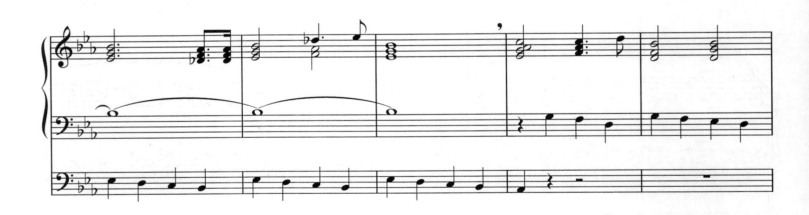

poco a poco cresc.

poco allargando

Broader

ff

simile

36

MOZZARELLA

39

Reduce

mf

Man.

43

POSTLUDE

PROCESSIONAL

SORTIE

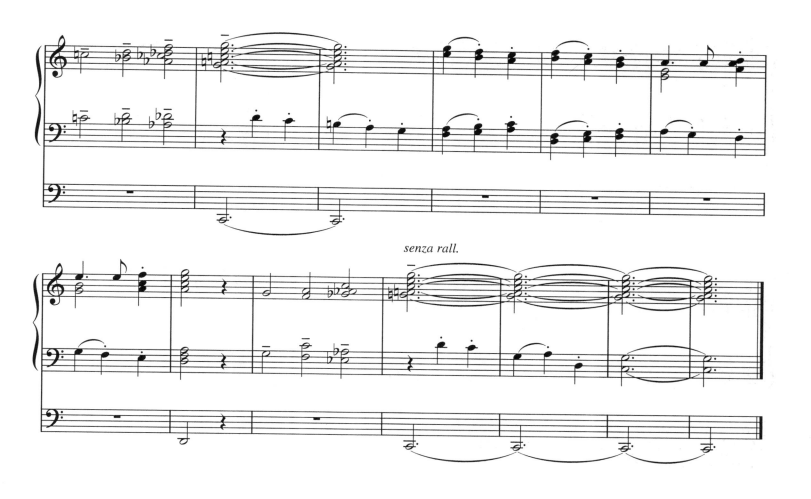

senza rall.